Piggy Monday

A TALE ABOUT MANNERS

SUZANNE BLOOM

www.av2books.com

Your AV² Media Enhanced book gives you a fiction readalong online. Log on to www.av2books.com and enter the unique book code from this page to use your readalong.

AV² Readalong Navigation

Go to **www.av2books.com**, and enter this book's unique code.

BOOK CODE

N 7 0 0 2 7 3

AV² by **Weigl** brings you media enhanced books that support active learning.

First Published by

ALBERT WHITMAN & COMPANY
Publishing children's books since 1919

HIGHLIGHTED TEXT

HOME

CLOSE

START READING

TITLE INFORMATION

PAGE TURNING

PAGE PREVIEW

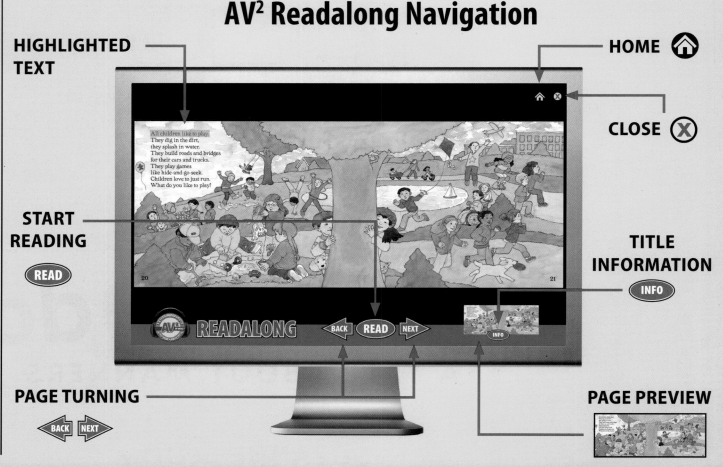

Published by AV² by Weigl
350 5ᵗʰ Avenue, 59ᵗʰ Floor New York, NY 10118
Websites: www.av2books.com   www.weigl.com

Printed in the United States of America in North Mankato, Minnesota
1 2 3 4 5 6 7 8 9 0   18 17 16 15 14

042014
WEP080414

Library of Congress Control Number: 2014937148

ISBN 978-1-4896-2365-2 (hardcover)
ISBN 978-1-4896-2366-9 (single user eBook)
ISBN 978-1-4896-2367-6 (multi-user eBook)

Text copyright ©2001 by Suzanne Bloom.
Illustrations copyright ©2001 by Suzanne Bloom.
Published in 2001 by Albert Whitman & Company.

On Monday,

Mrs. Hubbub's class was getting out of line.
She told them to behave or they would all turn into swine.

No one paid attention. Mike began to tease.

No one shared, took turns, or helped, and nobody said "please."

The children still were wiggly, until they heard a wail:
Amanda took Melinda's seat, and then she grew a tail!

In music, it was noted,
Sara wouldn't sing the song.
She was busy whispering,
and then her ears grew long.

At playground as the teams
picked sides,
they tried to leave Tom out.
Meanwhile Tommy picked
his nose and found he'd
grown a snout.

Lunchtime was chaotic. Everyone was rude.
No one used their silverware, and George was throwing food.

Stevie used his sleeve when he was wiping off his face.
Suddenly, his hand was gone — a hoof was in its place.

At rest time Mrs. Hubbub said, "I've told you more than once. Good manners are important." But all she heard was grunts.

Nurse Judy took their temperatures and gave their tails a twist.
"It's no ordinary flu," she said. "We need a specialist!"

The secretaries knew just who, and in a snap they dialed her.
"Pig Lady, will you help us, please, before it gets much wilder?"

She came as fast as soda fizz and asked the principal where she'd find the rude and rowdy class that doesn't care or share.

She lined them up and checked them out. She peered into their eyes, chucked their chinny-chin-chins and said, "This comes as no surprise.

"You've forgotten all your manners. In fact, you've gone hog-wild.
But together we can fix it." The piglets slowly smiled.

"Good manners are like magic. Everyone can learn
to treat each other with respect and be respected in return.

"Now let's get rid of those tails and ears. Blow your snouts and
dry your tears. It's really up to you, my dears:
Can you remember your manners?"

"When I get picked on,"
Tommy said,
"it makes me feel so small.
So don't make fun of anyone.
Don't bully or name-call."

"We close our mouths,"
said Ashley,
"when we eat our food,
because it's just disgusting
to see what's being chewed!"

Kevin had a good idea:
"Take turns — the game goes faster.
If we fight and break the rules,
it's a big disaster."

"In the old days, when
I wanted something, I would
just say 'gimme.'
Now I know that saying 'please'
is more polite," said Jimmy.

"You never play with me," Melinda said, "and it's no fun.
It feels so bad to be left out. I'd play with everyone."

Sara said, "We're sorry for ignoring you all day."
Then Amanda added, "Stay with us and play."

"I'll share my toys," said Keisha,
"if you're careful and don't break them.
But ask me for permission first, before you go
and take them."

Rebecca nodded, then she said, "It's up to us, I guess,
to put away the toys we use and clean up all our mess."

"I hold doors open," George announced, "and then say,
'After you.'
It really shocks the socks off people passing through."

"Excuse me, please! Excuse me, please!" said Jess.
"I'd like to mention
that when you say, 'Excuse me, please,' people
pay attention."

"I get it!" Erica declared. "We hurt each other's feelings!
We were bossy, mean, and rude. That's why
we started squealing."

"You've done it, dearies! I'm impressed.
You've progressed from worst to best.
You thought your way through an awful mess. Yes.
You recalled your manners."

Tails began to disappear. Ears shrank back to small.
Pig Lady shook each hand and said, "I'm so proud of you all."

Mrs. Hubbub thanked her as hooves
turned back to toes.
The children and the principal
were sad to see her go.

"I'm happy to have helped," she said.
"And though I'd love to stay,
there's another school nearby that needs me right away."

The class lined up for snack time.
There was juice in every cup.
No one hogged the muffins, and everyone cleaned up.

"Excuse me," "please," and "thank you" were heard
throughout the day.
Justin shared with Jesse, and Jake said, "Kev, let's play."

Whitney whispered, "Amber, you color very well."
And no one had a reason to shout "I'm gonna tell!"

The librarian was pleased to see the books
put on the shelves.

In art class Mike and Erica did not paint themselves.

At bus time Mrs. Hubbub waved
to every boy and girl,
blew a kiss and said, "There goes
the best class in the world!"

Yes, manners are like magic:
whether you're small or big,
be sure to always use them,
so you won't become a pig.